The

ELF

and the

FALLEN
OAK

Davina Sheckell

ISBN 979-8-89043-759-4 (paperback)
ISBN 979-8-89043-760-0 (digital)

Christian Faith Publishing
832 Park Avenue
Meadville, PA 16335
www.christianfaithpublishing.com

Printed in the United States of America

CHAPTER 1

As I walk down the forested mountain path, the birds sing a lovely song. I hear a gentle waterfall ahead, welcoming me underneath it for a quick afternoon shower. There are no voices, no blacksmith tools clanging, and no sounds except for the soft forest noises. Kuratakka birds swoop through the air just under the canopy of tree limbs above me, calling to each other in the gentle shadows. The beauty of the afternoon is enchanting.

I round a bend in the dirt path and come face-to-face with the waterfall that I have been hearing. I smell its earthy, mossy scent, and once again, it beckons me to step beneath its silvery white waters. However, I cannot take the time today. I am walking to the nearby village of Yfiil in search of a proper florist. I am fifteen years old, and this is the first time my mother has allowed me to leave my village, Kaahl, without supervision. If I am not back by sundown, I will probably be punished.

My oldest sister, Gwen, is getting married in a few weeks' time, and Kaahl does not have a proper

1

florist. There is no chance that Gwen will be married without flowers. My mother and Gwen are too busy working on gowns for the wedding to find a florist, and my younger sister is too small for such a trip. Hence the adventure of Lady Haléndal entering the forest alone!

All right. Perhaps I am not a lady, but a lass can dream, no? Many of the lords and ladies I have seen dress beautifully and eat well, yet they still have time for adventure. Seems to be a delightful life.

I continue down the pathway toward Yfíil, kicking small stones as I go. Little do I realize that my cheerful and untroubled attitude is about to change.

I see a movement ahead beside the path and frown. What is that? As I draw nearer to the source of the movement, my heart slowly begins to fill with dread. In all his brown-haired, pointed-eared, strong-bodied majesty, it is a forest elf, and he is injured.

The elf's leg is pinned beneath a fallen tree trunk, though I do not understand how. The tree did not rot and fall on its own; it was cut down not long ago, though no tools are in sight. How has this happened?

I hesitate for a moment at the center of the path. I have only seen forest elves a few times. Unlike the elves from the regions of the Opaakyi Sea, forest elves are large and strong. Rumor has it that they are unfriendly and unkempt, unwilling to rise from their cave homes in the forested mountains to live in modern stone or wood homes. They have been known to attack villages at random, taking anything they can and leaving death and pain behind them as they return to the forest. Most people stay as far from them as possible when they come to trade in Kaahl.

I realize, though, as I watch the young man struggle to free his leg, that I cannot simply leave him here out of fear of what he may do. I must help him. I also notice that he has already seen me.

The elf follows me with his eyes as I approach him. He studies my clothing as I study his. I am wearing a simple brown dress with puffed sleeves and laces on the front. The elf's clothing looks as though it were sewn from leaves and mosses, though I do not see how that is possible. Leaves die when they are no longer attached to a tree's branches.

"You look uncomfortable," I say to the young man.

I realize his cheeks are wet, as though he has been crying. Is he in pain? This tree must be very heavy.

The elf says nothing, and I remember that the forest elves don't speak my language. I look around for something to help me move the tree. A sturdy branch will do. Eventually, I find one. I shove it underneath the fallen tree trunk and brace it against another severed tree. Someone has been chopping down several trees in the area.

I push down on the branch with all my might. Nothing happens. I grit my teeth and try again, with the same result. I turn and sit on the sturdy branch, hoping that my full weight will help. The trunk barely moves.

I study the situation, thinking hard. Then I warily move to the strange elf's side. I sit near him, my back to the trunk, and brace my feet against the nearest stump. I push with my feet, shoving the trunk hard with my back. It moves a little.

The elf grits his teeth and lets out a small groan of pain.

I push harder. The trunk moves more, and the young man scrambles backward, finally freeing his leg and foot.

He clenches his jaw and curls into a ball as if to protect his leg. He moans in pain again, and I see that he is shaking.

I stand and touch his shoulder gently.

He snaps his head up to look at me, his eyes wide and full of tears of pain.

I realize then how green his eyes are—nearly the exact color of the grass he is sitting on. It is an odd color, but it suits him. I point to the leg and squat beside him.

He reluctantly lets me look at it.

The leg is bent at an awkward angle and clearly broken.

I look around for a good branch to brace the leg with. I find one, then search for something with which to tie it to the leg. I find nothing. I can feel the man's eyes following me as I move about the trees. I look back at him. I cannot simply leave him here. I must help.

My father was a physician before he died last year. I have helped him set many bones in the past. I know what I am doing, but I have no suitable vine, rope, or bandage to tie the brace to the leg.

I hesitate as an idea enters my mind. It is an awkward one, but it should work. I turn away from the elf, reach underneath the edge of my dress, and grasp the hem of my long slip. I pull, and it comes down. I step through it and return to the man, doing my best to ignore my burning cheeks.

"My father was a physician," I tell him, unsure how many words he can understand. "I have helped him set broken bones many times. I will help you."

I continue to talk soothingly to him, telling him what to expect as I tear strips of cloth from the cream-colored slip. Then I set the bone.

The elf screams and collapses backward, nearly losing consciousness. I brace his leg, wrapping the slip material around the leg to hold the strong, straight branch in place. It works. I step back, satisfied with my work. Father would be pleased.

I look at the elf's face. His eyes are closed, and his shoulders are shaking a bit as he works to contain his sobs. As big and strong as he is, he feels pain as much as we humans do.

I find yet another branch for the young man to use as a walking stick and pull leaves and thin twigs from it, giving him time to manage the pain on his own. Then I return and hold my hand out to him. I'm not sure if I am strong enough to help him stand, but I am willing to try.

The elf stares at my hand for a long time. Then he wipes tears from his face and clasps my hand. I use my other hand to grasp a nearby tree and pull.

With great care, the young elf staggers to his feet—his one good foot. He looks down at his brace and then back at me. There is silence. Neither of us knows what to do at this moment.

"Thank you."

The elf's words sound strange, as though he is trying to form them at the back of his throat and, at the same time, putting too much emphasis on his consonants. But he spoke my language. That is all I need.

I smile at him. "You're welcome." I hand him the makeshift staff. "Use this to help you walk."

He takes the stick and nods. He reaches out then and touches one of my blonde curls that has escaped the plaits on the back of my head.

I am reminded that all forest elves have only brown hair. The elf has probably never been close enough to a blonde human to touch his or her hair. I am tempted to touch the pointed tips of his ears in return, but I restrain myself.

I realize how young he looks. I have been thinking of him as a young man, but he appears to be not much older than I am. He is handsome, in a rough and brawny sort of way.

He gives me a small smile and turns away, waving as he disappears into the mountain forest.

I heave a sigh of relief. For someone believed to be cruel and frightening, the forest elf seemed appreciative.

I look at the freshly cut trees and wonder again how the elf managed to be trapped underneath one. Did someone chop down the tree and simply leave the injured elf trapped beneath it? That makes no sense...unless the elf tried to attack whoever was chopping the trees down.

I shiver at that thought and continue down the path toward Yfíil. I need to find a florist. That should be my focus. However, as the day continues its course, I find those strangely green eyes invading my thoughts.

CHAPTER 2

A few hours later, I return to Kaahl before sundown as planned. I enter my home to find mountains of fabrics on the table, floor, and even one chair. Gwen is sitting underneath the fabric on the chair, working hard on a gown for my youngest sister, Leah, to wear at the wedding. Right now, Leah is wearing a nightgown, playing with her rag doll beside the fireplace.

Having seen me coming, Mother is filling a bowl with soup from the pot hanging over the fire. She shoves a pile of green fabric aside and places the bowl on the table. "Haléndal, you're home. I kept the soup warm for you."

I shiver as I move to the table. "Thank you, Mother. Warm soup will be welcomed, as the evening has become quite chilly."

I sit and say a blessing over my food as Mother fills a glass with water for me.

"Were you successful?" she asks. "Gwen has been rather stressed about her wedding flowers."

Gwen laughs from her seat beneath the billowy green gown. "I believe you have been more stressed about the entire wedding than I have, Mother."

Mother winks at me.

I smile. "I was, though Yfiil's florist is more expensive than I had imagined. I gave him the money I had and promised him both a goat and the next two hatched chickens."

Mother taps her fingers on the table, thinking. She does not appear happy about this decision. Her silence makes me nervous. I know I threw the second chicken into the deal on a whim when the florist appeared hesitant. I could have chosen some smaller bouquets, but I had fallen in love with the larger ones instead and insisted on purchasing them. I am rethinking that commitment because we have only recently started raising chickens for eggs and meat. Giving up two this soon could be a bad decision.

"You will love the bouquets, Mother," I say, hoping to redeem myself. "The flowers will be beautiful. You won't regret the cost."

Mother sighs. "I hope not."

The next two weeks pass in a flurry of activities. Work and wedding preparations surround my family. There are a few quiet moments in which I wonder if I should tell my mother or our village head about the elf I helped in the forest. I do not know where he came from. If his elven dwelling is nearby, his people could become a problem for ours. However, I am nervous about mentioning the elf to anyone. Since he was grateful and kind to me, I do not want my village leaders searching for his people. Perhaps I should just leave things as they are.

Before we know it, the wedding day arrives. Gwen's flowers are lovely, just as gorgeous as the sample bouquet when I traveled to Yfiil. I am thrilled—absolutely thrilled!

More importantly, Gwen is excited as well. She runs from table to arch to fencepost, her excitement overflowing at the sight of the fabulous white roses and bright green leaves. Then she sweeps me up in a giant hug.

"Oh, thank you, Haléndal! These are truly the most beautiful bouquets I have ever seen!"

I laugh gleefully. "I'm glad you like them. Now let us get you into your gown before Rowan sees you!"

An hour later, we are at the ceremony. Mother, Leah, and I, along with Gwen's closest friend Heather, are standing near Gwen. We are wearing gorgeous green gowns with full skirts and white lace covering the bodices.

The bride outshines us all in her fabulous white dress, with a skirt so big that I must flatten it to hug her. Gwen looks beautiful, with dark curls framing her face and her hair swept into an intricate updo that took our mother two hours to make.

We stand in the village square, waiting for the groom to make his appearance. Each of us in green gowns got to spend time with Rowan this morning, offering what advice we could. That is our people's custom. I have no marriage experience, so I simply told him to always treat Gwen as he already has, buying her gifts and caring passionately for her. I hope it wasn't silly advice.

A moment later, the music sounds, and the smiling groom appears, coming down the street toward us. He is surrounded by children singing songs and carrying sweet spices and perfumes, a gift from Rowan's family for the bride. Leah runs to join them. As soon as Rowan reaches to take Gwen's hand, though, we hear a scream.

It is a distant scream, but heads turn, looking for the source of the sound. More screaming comes, followed by wailing. Whispers scatter throughout the crowd as people fidget nervously. Some men and women leave the ceremony, searching for the source of the scream.

In short order, one man returns, his face as white as my sister's wedding gown. "Forest elves!" he pants. "Probably two hundred of them! I…I was not aware that any lived near our village!"

My heart stops. I never told anyone about my encounter with the elf caught under the fallen tree. I was afraid. Now I fear that I could have stopped this.

Immediately, our village head, who was about to perform the wedding, stands up tall. "Parents, take your children to the nearest homes. Fathers and mothers who know how to fight, surround the buildings and protect them with your lives. Anyone else who has skill with the sword must stand here in the village square and fight. This is the easiest place for a battle, as there is more space for fighting. We outnumber them nearly two to one." He continues giving orders as everyone scatters to execute his hurried plan.

Mother grabs Leah's hand and motions for me to follow her to the nearest house. I shake my head. I have been training with the sword for quite some time now. Many people in our village began learning to fight with a sword at a young age, and my adventurous spirit would not let me rest until I had discovered my potential.

Mother's eyes widen. "Haléndal, come with me. Please! You are too young and cannot fight in such a billowy gown."

I run toward my home instead, which is nearer the edge of the village. "I'm retrieving my sword!" I shout at her.

Mother does not argue anymore. She does not have time. She needs to get Leah to safety.

I enter our home and immediately remove the big dress that I have been wearing. I rush toward the bedroom in my corset and slip, nearly dying of embarrassment when the front door swings open and Gwen and Rowan enter. I scoot quickly from the room, hoping that I was not seen.

I kick the door shut and pull a random dress from the closet to wear. As I pull it over my head, I hear my sister and her betrothed arguing in the main room.

"Gwen, you need to stay here. I need you to be safe."

"Rowan, I cannot stay here and let everyone else take risks. I won't stay and hide while everyone else fights for our village and our people!"

"But Gwen, you are wearing an enormous gown! How can you possibly fight in that?"

My sister is silent. I feel her pain. Gwen's dress has so many buttons up the back it would take an eternity to unfasten them all. She cannot simply pull the dress over her head as I did mine.

"I'll help her out of it," I offer, reappearing in my new dress, sword in hand. "It will take a while, though."

I suddenly remember my belt and scabbard and lunge back into the bedroom to retrieve them. As I step back toward the main room, I hear voices. I poke my head out the bedroom door to see big, strong, brown-haired men and women entering our house.

They are forest elves, speaking a strange language I cannot understand. Rowan pulls his sword from its scabbard and takes on two elves at once. I watch him fight in awe. I know he is good with his sword, but I have rarely seen what he can do. I am transfixed by his skill.

At the same time, I wonder where elves get their swords. Do they craft swords in their cave homes?

"Haléndal! Go! Find help!"

I turn to the side to find Gwen doing her best to fight three more elves who have come in through the door…and more are still coming. My heart sinks. I do not know when or where she grabbed her sword, but it will do her no good. Gwen will never be able to keep the brutes at bay. Neither will I. The idea of leaving Gwen and Rowan here alone makes me feel nauseated, but Gwen is right. I must find help.

Quickly, before I am seen, I sprint across the bedroom and climb through the open window. I feel like a coward as I escape into the sunlight. I desperately hope my sister won't… Well, I hope I still *have* a sister when I return with help.

CHAPTER 3

The sounds of swords clashing behind me cease. I was going to run behind our neighbor's home, but now I wonder what is happening inside. Is Gwen all right? What about Rowan? My fear seizes control of my logic, and I slip quietly toward the street in front of the house. Elves are running in and out of homes, pulling humans out with them. Others are moving toward the square, where I can hear more sword fighting. How has a wedding turned out to be so chaotic and terrifying?

Reaching the edge of the street, I hide in the shadows and peer around the corner of my house. Gwen and Rowan are dragged out into the street, their swords in the hands of their foes. Blessedly, they are alive. I do see fewer elves coming out of my house than I saw enter it. I wonder if that means there are elven corpses in our main room. The idea makes me shiver.

I suddenly notice a young male elf sitting on a wooden crate in the middle of the street. His leg is stretched out in front of him, wrapped, and braced.

It is the elf that I helped in the forest. The elves are bringing the humans they find to the young elf. He shakes his head at every man brought to him, and then the humans are tied with vines from the forest and are left sitting in their doorways. What in this kingdom is happening?

Presently, Rowan and Gwen are shoved toward the elf in the street. The elf's eyes widen, and he points at Rowan. "*Esh minettè! Minettè quaii iss bruffónn!*"

I have no idea what he said.

The elf behind Rowan hits him on the back of his head with the pommel of Rowan's own sword. Rowan grunts in pain and falls to his knees.

I need to get help. I know this. However, I feel rooted to the spot, watching and wondering what will happen to my sister and her betrothed.

The young elf in the street waves his hand at Gwen in a dismissive manner, but a large elf steps from the crowd to stand near him, speaking in the strange language of the elves and pointing at my sister. The large elf has similar features to the injured one but is older, with a full brown beard. He also has a green gemstone that is somehow set into his forehead. Perhaps this is the injured elf's father?

"*Niggf!*" the younger elf says, shaking his head.

I assume the word he said means no.

The young elf continues talking with the older one. They appear to be in an argument, with angry expressions and curt hand movements. I gasp as the elf with a beard backhands the younger one on the side of his head. He points to the gemstone on his forehead and shouts something again.

The younger elf winces and says one more clipped, angry word. He then spits at the older elf's feet, but there is no more arguing.

Rowan and Gwen's hands are bound behind their backs, and I realize with a twist of my heart that they will be taken away.

I turn and run back through the space between my house and the one next to it. I weave through houses and shops until I reach the village square. Swords clash all around me, both elven and human. Bodies bestrew the ground, some injured, some dead. I have to fight down bile at the sight.

A tall, muscular, elven woman with a sword rushes toward me. I pull my sword from its scabbard and meet her attack. We fight. I concentrate hard, trying to recall all the lessons I have learned over the years. The woman is larger than I am, and she is vicious, yet her skills with the sword are secondary to mine and ineffective. In a couple of minutes, I pierce her through.

I stare at her body on the ground and the blood flowing from the wound in her chest. Never before have I slain another person! The sight of her corpse makes me taste bile again.

Settle yourself, Haléndal! I think. *This is a part of war. You brought this on yourself by running for your sword and not listening to Mother.*

I hear a sound to my right, and I instinctively spin out of the way as a sword swishes across the spot where I was standing. The elven man holding the sword mutters something and regains his balance, attempting another slice. I meet his attack. His sword-fighting abilities far surpass the woman's. I find myself in retreat, never finding an opportunity for a counterattack.

The powerful elf presses in with blow after blow, and as I struggle to block each one, I suddenly hear a strange horn blowing. The sound is loud. Whoever blew it must be standing nearby, perhaps somewhere in the village square. The horn startles and distracts me, making me unable to block the elf's next strike effectively. I deflect it as best I can, but his blade slices into the skin of my upper right arm.

I cry out in pain and stumble backward, nearly dropping my sword. I have not been injured often in practice. It is difficult to duplicate injuries in training.

I pull my sword back up, trying to ignore the pain and the blood dripping down my arm. I am fully expecting the elf to take advantage of my weakness and cut me down.

However, he hesitates, stepping away from me instead and looking at something behind me. I need to see what is behind me, but I cannot turn my head, or I could be dead in the next second.

I make a quick decision. I spin to the side and raise my sword again, taking a glance in the direction his eyes were looking. To my surprise, the battle is slowing down. The elves are leaving the square as if in retreat. The horn must have been calling them to leave, though I do not understand why. We have only been fighting for a short time.

My opponent snarls something at me in his language. He then stoops to pick up the woman I killed a moment ago, carrying her body as he leaves.

I am tempted to get revenge for the slice in my arm, but I don't. I will not stab him in the back as he cares for the body of his dead accomplice. I watch as the square empties of elves, even of elven corpses. No elf is left behind, whether dead or alive.

I work my way through the confused crowd to the village head, Kenton. I shout his name, and he turns to look at me. His hair is dark with sweat, and he looks as though he has been fighting much more than I have. He looks weary, and there is blood running down the side of his face from a small cut near his left eye.

"They took Rowan and Gwen!" I say. "I tried to come and tell you, but I was delayed and forced to fight. They bound them up and took them! They also left many people bound and sitting on the thresholds of their homes."

Kenton mutters something under his breath. He turns to a man nearby, ordering him to arrange a group of men and women to search for the elven dwellings.

I tell him on which street to find the fettered people, and then I hurry that way to see if I can help. When the search party leaves, I will doubtless be going with them. My sister's life is at stake.

I am the first person to come to my street. I fully intended to help release the poor men and women who were left sitting in their doorways, but now I see something that catches my eye. There is movement in the street near the edge of the village. I instantly realize it is the elf that I helped in the forest a couple of weeks ago. He is moving away, leaning hard on the walking stick I gave him.

I run toward him and shout, "Hey!"

His head whips around to look at me, and his eyes widen with recognition. He quickly turns into the space between two houses, obviously hoping to find a place to hide.

There is no way that an elf hobbling on a broken leg is going to outrun me. I sprint down the street and dash between the houses. The elf is moving surprisingly fast, despite the pain he must be experiencing.

"Stop!" I shout.

The elf finally gives up on attempting to flee and turns around, his face showing pain, frustration, and…something else. Is it fear that I see in his eyes? Or perhaps regret?

I rush upon him with all the wrath of an enraged dragon. He has every reason in the kingdom to be afraid of me!

The elf tries to step away from me, but I run straight into him, shoving his large frame so hard that he stumbles backward and falls. He screams through clenched teeth and clutches his leg with both hands. Sweat beads on his forehead.

"What is wrong with you?" he hisses angrily.

His words are heavily accented, but he knows my language better than I realized.

"Where is my sister?" I demand. "Where's Rowan? Where did your people take them?"

He gives some kind of disgusted snort. "I cannot tell you that! It is our home. Your people will kill us if you find our dwellings."

I scowl at him. "And what did your people just do to mine?"

I continue when he does not answer, "They invaded our village and killed us—unprovoked! We did nothing to you! We were trading peacefully with your kind but a few weeks ago. Now you are terrorizing us!"

The elf glares at me. "I am uncertain what *unprovoked* means, but I tell the truth. That man is the one who left me under the tree in the forest!"

CHAPTER 4

I stare at him in shock. "What? Rowan? You're a lunatic! Rowan would never do that!"

I realize, however, with a twinge of dread, that Rowan does have a mean temper. I firmly believe that he would never harm Gwen, but he was once well-known for getting into fights in the tavern. Thankfully, that is in the past. Rowan stopped drinking months ago and has been doing well. But he still angers easily. It is something that he has been working on.

The elf shakes his head and says, "I remember that face and hair. It is him. I know this."

"Well…," I start, trying to come up with a coherent question, "why? What made him decide to do that?"

The elf makes a slight movement to sit more comfortably, but he groans in pain as he moves. I almost feel guilty for hurting his injured leg…almost.

He runs a hand through his earth-brown strands of hair. "You would not understand. You are a human."

I resist the urge to kick him. "Then help me understand! You took my sister and the man she was marrying! You took them from their wedding!"

The elf squints at me in confusion. "Wedding? What is—wedding?"

"They were getting married! A wedding is a marriage ceremony."

He thinks for a moment. "Is that why she was wearing the big...clothing?" He uses his hands to express how billowy Gwen's gown is.

"Yes! Why else?"

He shrugs. "My father thought she was important. That is why he took her. We only came to get—how do you say it in your language?—*revenge*. That is all. I remembered that you helped me in the forest and came from this way. I tried to tell them not to hurt anyone since you showed kindness to me. I did not want a battle. Father insisted." He spits on the ground bitterly, and I am reminded of the argument I witnessed some minutes ago.

"Wait a minute," I say, my mind racing. "So, your father took her because he believed her to be someone important? And the big white gown made him think she was important?"

"Gown?" the elf questions.

"Clothing," I clarify.

He nods. "Yes. Father wanted to send a warning by taking someone he believed to be a leader in your village."

I understand now. His words make sense, though I still cannot imagine Rowan trapping someone underneath a tree and leaving him there. "Why did Rowan trap you under the tree?"

"I told you that you would not understand. You are a—"

His words are cut off as I kick him in the side. He grunts and scowls at me.

"What is wrong with you?" he asks again.

"I need to know!" I say. "I cannot imagine Rowan doing such a thing."

The elf studies my face for a long time, saying nothing and thinking.

As I wait, I realize that time is slipping away. Every moment I stand here, Gwen and Rowan are taken farther from me. I huff and turn away, unsure of what to do. I have a sword; the elf does not. I cannot hurt him, though. If what he says is true, he was only trying to find and take Rowan because of the great wrong the man had done. The elf said that he had not wanted the fighting, and I saw him arguing with his father over whether or not to take Gwen. My mind whirls and scatters in a thousand directions. How do I get my sister and her betrothed back?

"We need those trees," the elf says, his voice quiet.

I turn back to him. "What?"

"We need them." The elf stares at the ground as if mentioning this fact is humbling in some way. "Chinífia trees provide life for our people. We always live near chinífia trees. If the trees are cut down, or if they start to die, our people start to die. We move when a grove of chinífia trees starts to die off or gets cut down."

I stand in silence, thinking. I remember now that the trees in the area where I freed the young elf's leg were different from those nearby. I believe we call them oak trees. The forest near our village has a wide range of unique trees, from oak to aspen to evergreen. I am unsure how the forest grows in such a way, but it is unique and beautiful.

The elf continues, "I was walking in the forest, and I came upon…*Rowan*…chopping down the trees." He stumbles a bit over Rowan's name, which is unfamiliar to him. "I tried to talk to him. I detest telling humans of our need for those trees. We have done so in the past, only to have an entire village of human men come and cut down the whole grove near our home. We lost twenty-three of our people in only a few days before we discovered another grove of chinífia trees." He pauses and shakes his head, still staring at the ground.

It is strange to see him this humble after the scowls and glares I have received thus far in the conversation. I do not blame him for trying to avoid telling humans the source of their lives if what he says is true.

The elf continues to tell me his story, finally looking up at me. He says that he walked near Rowan, intending to tell him about the elves' need for the trees. He had not wanted to tell him this, but he was unsure how else to convince Rowan to cut down other trees instead. However, as soon as

Rowan saw the elf, he raised his axe at him, not letting him come any closer. The elf told Rowan of the trees' importance, but Rowan only seemed to become frustrated. Rowan said some things that the elf did not understand and started chopping again. The elf lunged forward and grabbed Rowan's arm, trying to stop him. They struggled for a bit. Even though the elf was larger, Rowan's past fighting experiences gave him an advantage. He shoved the elf down and took one last swing at the tree, severing the trunk from the stump. It fell, and though the elf tried to scramble away, the enormous tree landed on his leg. Rowan looked surprised and stared at the elf as if trying to decide what to do. Rowan had not intended for the tree to land on the elf. After a moment's hesitation, however, Rowan walked away in spite of the fact that the elf was calling for him to come back.

I stare at the elf for a few moments after he finishes his story. His eyes beg for me to believe him.

"I did not want the fighting," he insists again. "I simply wanted Rowan. I knew my people would want revenge once they heard what happened. What is that human saying? 'An eye for an eye'?"

"All right," I say finally. "I believe you...but how do we get them back?"

The elf almost laughs. "You cannot! My father will never allow it!"

"Is your father the...elven village head?" I ask.

"He is called our elder," the elf corrects me. "Yes, he is our leader."

"What will he do to them?"

"They will become his servants."

"Slaves," I find myself correcting him, a bitter edge to my voice.

He shrugs. "They will serve him, so they are servants."

I roll my eyes. I know it is a childish gesture, but I am frustrated with the situation.

"What is your name?" I suddenly ask.

He hesitates, looking into my eyes. "I am called Lifií."

It sounded like he said *leafy*. The name amuses me since he is wearing leafy clothing. The idea that anything would amuse me at all in this situation is... interesting.

"All right, Lifií," I say, "please listen to me. What Rowan did was absolutely wrong, but you must understand something. He is a woodworker. He makes things from wood and sells them—furniture and things of that nature. Oak is a strong wood, and he uses it to make tables and things."

"Oak?"

"That's our word for the trees you mentioned," I explain. "They are strong and make excellent furniture."

"Stone is stronger," Lifií says, confused. "Why cut down such...magnificent things—for a table? They are alive!"

I shake my head. "I did not come here to enter a philosophical discussion. I need to find my sister. You are wasting time!" I pause and take a deep breath.

"Rowan uses those trees for his livelihood. He uses any trees, for that matter. He simply did not want to lose them to you. He was startled when you approached him, and that is why he raised his axe at you. Leaving you under the tree was wrong—very, very wrong. When our village leaders find out what he did, I am certain he will be punished. Our leaders wish to keep the peace between your people and mine."

Lifií squints at me. "Your sister is not a village leader?"

"No! She was getting married to Rowan."

Lifií hesitates again. Then he slowly reaches out his hand to me. At that moment, he looks like a child reaching out to a parent, trusting that he will not be rejected.

He is correct.

I reach for the nearest thing I can find to brace myself, which happens to be a windowsill on the house beside me. I wrap my fingers around the sill and hang on tightly as I reach for his outstretched hand with my free one. I pull him up.

He sucks in a shaky breath as he stands. The fact that he is currently in intense pain is clear.

Guilt stabs me in the chest. I had every right to shove him as I did, but I still find myself apologizing.

"I'm sorry," I say, my voice quiet. "I did not intend to hurt you quite so much." The words are true.

Lifií glances at me and shrugs, though his face shows more pain than the shrug indicated. "We will go and retrieve your sister," he tells me. "I did not want to take her anyway. I do not agree with my father's methods."

"And what of Rowan?" I ask, feeling my heart sink.

"Rowan stays."

CHAPTER 5

Rowan stays. The elf's words sound final.

"What?" I exclaim. "No! Even though Rowan was incredibly insensitive to you and your people, he was trying to keep his livelihood, his craft. Perhaps after this incident, he will be more likely to treat your people better. Please, help! He cannot stay."

"He must pay for his actions," Lifií says, his voice firm. "Rowan stays."

"I told you I am certain that he will be punished by our leaders. Isn't that enough?"

Lifií scowls. "Isn't it enough that I will try to free your sister? Once my father finds out that I am responsible for her freedom, he will beat me. Freeing Rowan as well will make him even angrier. Rowan stays!"

I open my mouth to argue again, but I close it when I realize I am wasting more time. I will go with him to find Gwen, but I will not leave without Rowan.

"All right," I say, "I am coming with you."

Lifíí looks annoyed but does not argue. "Come quickly. My father will be wondering where I am. We must get to your sister before he realizes how long I have been gone."

I want to point out that "quickly" is not an option for us, as he has a broken leg, but I hold my tongue. I follow him as he moves slowly and painfully between buildings, keeping away from the street. Neither of us wants to be seen by my people. I have gained this elf's trust for the time being. If we are seen, I will be kept behind, and Kenton will send men with Lifíí. However, I know that Lifíí is only willing to do this for me because I am the girl who helped him in the forest.

We move away from the village and into the forest. I follow Lifíí through the trees, avoiding the main trails that my people often take. When we reach the grove of trees where I helped Lifíí a couple of weeks ago, I see that the area has not changed. No one removed the tree trunks that were cut down. I am unsure why. Perhaps Rowan did not want to come back and be reminded of his actions. Thankfully, several oak trees are still standing tall in the area.

We turn right and slip through the trees. After walking for a few minutes, Lifíí stops and leans on his staff. He is sweating, and his face is twisted with pain.

I touch his arm, and he looks at me.

"I'm sorry," I say again.

Lifíí shrugs. "I will not remember the broken leg when my father is finished with me."

"Will he honestly beat you?" I ask, my eyes wide.

I cannot imagine being beaten by a parent, but it is apparent that elves live their lives differently than we do. I cannot judge the elven ways simply because they seem cruel by human standards.

Lifií shrugs again and wipes sweat from his brow. He points to my right arm. "You are bleeding."

I look down at my arm. Blood is running down the upper arm and dripping off the elbow. Simply looking at the wound from my short swordfight with an elf makes me remember the pain. I wince. "Somehow, I forgot about this," I say. "It is all right, though. I will be fine."

Lifií shakes his head. He looks around and takes a moment to collect certain leaves, berries, and other things. He crumbles some things, mixes others, and tears a strip from his strange tunic. He then looks about for something with which to wipe the blood from my arm.

I use the hem of my dress to do so.

He raises an eyebrow at me but says nothing. He packs his leaf-and-berry mixture into the wound on my arm and wraps it with the torn tunic piece. He nods in satisfaction.

I look at the wound. It is still painful, but I am curious about what the concoction will do. I do not ask.

"Thank you," I say.

Lifií looks again at my face. His grass-green eyes are unreadable. We stare at each other for a moment.

He reaches out to touch a blonde curl that is damp with sweat and hanging over my eye, pushing it behind my ear. He then continues walking without saying another word. The next time I start to talk, Lifií motions for silence. We must be nearing the elven dwelling caves.

Moments later, he catches my attention and points. I follow the line of his finger but see nothing except a cliff and trees.

"Do you see that?" he asks me.

"See what?"

"Those trees and bushes are only imitations made by our finest craftsmen to cover our cave openings."

I try to look again. I do notice how some of the trees look a bit different from the others nearby. The opening to the cave must be past the false trees and underbrush in the cliff face.

I nod. "How do we get to my sister?"

"I have been thinking about this," Lifií says. "I believe my father will put her in the hole near his quarters."

I stare at him. "'The hole?' What does that mean? Will it be difficult to free her?"

"I have a plan." Lifií turns to look at me, his face serious. "The only way for this to work is for us to—what's the word?—*pretend* that you are another captive."

A cold chill runs through my body, and I shiver involuntarily. "A-another captive?" I whisper. "I...I do not know if..." I do not even have a coherent thought at the moment. What if this was all a ploy to take me captive as well?

Lifií puts a hand on my shoulder. Though his hand is large and rough, it is gentle. "I will not leave you in there." He places his other hand on his heart and moves it to his mouth and then to his forehead in a couple of swift motions. Is that supposed to mean something? He must see my confusion because he says, "That is our most honored promise." He makes the same quick motions. "It means that if I break my word, it will be your right to slay me."

I stare at him. Slay...meaning kill? "That is a serious promise," I say.

"Your sister must be freed. I will not take you in there as a servant. It will be a..." He searches for the correct word in my language.

"Trickery?" I offer.

"Um...perhaps. I do not know what that means."

"All right. A pretense then."

"That sounds right." Lifií nods. "Are you willing to go?"

I hesitate. Can this elf be trusted? Sometimes he acts angry with me, and other times he seems almost tender or sweet. I realize that the only way to help Gwen or Rowan without going back for help and starting another serious battle is to follow through with Lifií's plan. I take a deep breath.

"Let us go," I say, pointing toward the hidden cave entrance.

Lifíí looks impressed. He nods, then turns and uses a knife hanging from his belt to cut a vine from a nearby tree. "I must bind your wrists to make them believe me, and you must give me your sword."

I hesitate. This is one of the scariest things I have ever done. What if Lifíí is lying to me?

"I will not leave you here, leave you tied, or keep your sword." Lifíí makes the same peculiar motions with his hand once again. "I will get you back out of there even if it costs me my life. You helped me in the forest. I will not repay evil for kindness. Besides, even with my broken leg, I could have taken your sword if I had truly wanted it for myself."

I am unsure if I believe that. He appeared afraid of me in the village. That injured leg would undoubtedly be a hindrance. However, this does not matter. What matters is getting near Gwen. "All right," I agree, "bind me."

CHAPTER 6

I pull my sword from its scabbard and hold it out to Lifíí. He shakes his head and points to my belt and scabbard.

"All of it," he says.

I sigh and replace the sword. I then pull the belt off and hand it to him, along with the sword and the scabbard.

Lifíí gives me another impressed look. He seems unable to believe that I am brave enough to do this.

I dream of adventure, do I not? "Lady Haléndal," right? Here is the adventure. I am unsure if this is the adventure I have been dreaming of, but I will do it for Gwen and Rowan. Despite what he has done, Rowan must come home to his people. Kenton will decide what to do with him. Kenton will be strict with Rowan's punishment. Rowan will regret his actions if he does not already.

After Lifíí ties my hands behind my back, the vines much looser than they should have been, he takes my arm and pulls me toward the cave. While he was tying my hands, he told me that he would have to be a bit rough and that I must act scared and angry. That should not be too difficult to do. I *am* scared and angry.

As we near the cave, a male elf with tight brown braids covering his head steps through the false underbrush. His hand is on the hilt of his sword.

"Lifií," he says in confusion. He asks Lifií a question.

Lifií moves a bit, and I feel something sharp barely prick my back—Lifií's knife, I realize. When did he get the knife out? He has a short conversation with the elf in braids.

Sir Braids, as I name him in my head, finally nods and motions for us to follow him.

As he enters the cave behind the trees and shrubbery, I turn on a whim and pretend to attempt a panicked escape. Lifií catches my arm and twists it in a way that makes me cry out in pain. As he drags me back to stand before him, I see the pained look in his eyes. The movement hurt his injured leg. I regret my pretended escape attempt, but I know that it made what is happening appear more realistic.

Sir Braids leads us through dimly lit passageways and chambers, past many elves who stare at us with raised eyebrows. I keep my head down, not wanting to see the large, intimidating elves around me. Within a short time, at the end of a dimly lit corridor, I see a barred iron gate blocking the entrance of another underground chamber. A giant elf stands in front of it. Sir Braids motions toward Sir Giant and walks away. After another brief conversation with

Lifíí, Sir Giant unlocks the gate and pulls it open, his muscles bulging.

Lifíí shoves me hard through the gate, making me stumble and fall to the hard stone floor. Sir Giant kicks me farther into the small chamber, then closes the gate. Panic seizes me, and I look at Lifíí through the bars.

The young elf glances at Sir Giant, who is relocking the gate. While Sir Giant is distracted, Lifíí makes another quick series of hand motions, the ones he showed me in the forest. They set me at ease. I do not know if it is wise to trust this elf, but I do.

Lifíí hobbles away, leaning on his walking stick. I struggle to a sitting position and look around me. The chamber has no torches; only a bit of light comes from one torch set into the cave wall outside the gate. However, I see Gwen and Rowan sitting near the far wall. Both have vines keeping their arms tightly bound to their sides and a cloth shoved into their mouths. Their eyes widen as they recognize me.

Emotions flood through my body—both relief and apprehension. I scoot across the floor and whisper to them why I am here and that an elf has promised to help me. As I explain, I move until I can pull the rags from Rowan and Gwen's mouths.

Rowan stares at me. "You came here with an elf's promise of help? Haléndal, you cannot trust that elf! Forest elves are savage! They cannot be trusted."

Anger blazes through me, hot as fire. "Do you want me to talk about being savage? What about cutting down a tree that elves need to survive? Or perhaps leaving an elf trapped under an enormous tree trunk in the forest?"

Rowan's mouth gapes open. "What…? How…?"

"Haléndal!" Gwen scolds. "What in this kingdom are you talking about?"

"Rowan knows," I say, watching Rowan's facial expression in the dim lighting.

It is true. He looks pained and ashamed.

"Is…is that what this is for?" Rowan asks, eyes wide and full of regret and fear.

"Yes! They wanted revenge for what you did to that elf!"

There is silence for a few moments. Gwen again asks us what we are talking about, and this time Rowan explains, his head lowered in humility.

"I regret my actions every time I think about them," he says when he is finished, "but when I went back to make things right, the elf was gone."

"I found him and helped him on my way to Yfíil when I went to order flowers for the wedding," I say. "I never told anyone about him. I was afraid to. I did not know if I should or not. Now, I wish I had. If only…"

There is a commotion near the gate. We look up to see the elven elder looking at us through the iron bars. His son is standing beside him, and they are deep in conversation. Well, truthfully, it appears to be another argument, though the two elves do not appear to be as angry as they were during the first argument that I witnessed.

I lower my head, but I watch out of the corner of my eye. The elder does not seem to notice that Rowan and Gwen are missing the cloths that were in their mouths a short while ago. The elder eventually nods his head at Lifií and walks away. Lifií looks at me, and I long to see him make his oath motions again before walking away, but he does not. I assume this is because Sir Giant still stands outside the gate, guarding us.

The afternoon turns into evening, and as the torches outside our prison start going out, Sir Giant is replaced by Lifií. I am surprised that Lifií is allowed to be a guard with his broken leg. He needs to rest and give the leg some time to heal. The elves must have confidence that we cannot escape through the iron gate because they allow an injured man to guard us.

Time passes, and the caverns become still in the night. The elves must be resting. We no longer hear voices calling to each other, tools, or anything else. There is only silence.

Lifií slides down to a sitting position outside the gate and stares at us through the bars. His expression is unreadable.

Rowan cannot look at the elf. He keeps his head down in shame. Eventually, he can no longer contain his mortification. He slides across the prison floor and raises his head to look at Lifií.

"I am told your name is Lifií," he says, using the name that I whispered to him as we were being watched by Sir Giant.

Rowan continues, "I cannot even begin to describe my great shame and regret for the pain I caused you. I am truly and deeply sorry."

Lifií simply stares at Rowan, his expression indiscernible. He appears still angry, but it is hard to know for certain. The torch on the wall has yet to go out entirely, but it is much dimmer than earlier, making it difficult to see Lifií's expression well.

Rowan lowers his head again. "I have no right to ask anything of you, but if I may humbly make one request, I would ask you to please free Gwen. She has done nothing amiss. Haléndal has told me that you wish me to stay and serve your father as retribution for leaving you under the tree when it fell on you." Rowan raises his head once more. "I will willingly stay if my betrothed and the lass Haléndal may return to Kaahl. Please, Lifií, allow the women to go free."

Lifií clenches his jaw, and then he pushes to his feet with much pain. He hobbles to the gate, leans on his walking stick, and stares down at Rowan.

Rowan gulps and scoots away from the gate as though the intimidating elf might somehow harm him through the bars.

Lifií speaks to Rowan for the first time. "I made a Rajuntiis Oath to the young Haléndal, as you have called her. I believe you would call it a life oath. It is our most honored promise. I will not break my word."

He glances down the empty corridor and lowers his voice. "I will do my best to free the women, but you must remain behind." He gives Rowan a hard look as if daring him to refuse.

Rowan simply nods, though he also lowers his head. "Thank you. We are indebted to you."

Lifií shakes his head and points at me. "I am indebted to her. She has more kindness in her soul than you will have for as long as you live."

Lifií pauses and turns his head, watching and listening for movement in the caves. All is silent. He pulls a key from his belt, unlocks the gate, and pulls it. He winces in pain and must adjust his stance as he pulls the heavy iron gate. His muscles bulge.

The gate's hinges make a creaking noise that seems deafening in the quiet cave.

Lifií freezes and looks down the corridor, waiting and listening. We wait a long time, sweat beading on our foreheads, but no one comes. Lifií pulls the door again, and it opens without a sound this time. With one more look down the passage, he steps into our prison, where Rowan, Gwen, and I sit on the floor, still bound with strong vines. He pulls his knife from his belt and looks at me.

I realize that with his broken leg, he cannot crouch beside me to cut my bonds. I scoot backward until my back is against the wall, then push myself up to a standing position. Lifií cuts the vines binding my wrists, and I move my arms, grateful for the mobility. My bonds were loose and only on my wrists. I cannot imagine how my sister and Rowan must feel with their arms tightly bound to their sides.

I help Gwen to her feet. She is still wearing her wedding gown, and Lifií must press his body into the large ruffles and layers of the skirt to be close enough to cut the vines binding her.

As she rubs feeling back into her arms and wrists, my heart races. I promised myself that I would not leave without Rowan. I need to keep my promise. I *will* keep my promise.

CHAPTER 7

As Lifií moves his knife back to his belt, I reach out with one quick movement and strike his knife hand, knocking the knife to the ground with a clatter. I stoop and retrieve the knife, moving quickly away from Lifií, who cannot move as swiftly as I can.

Gwen gasps, and Lifií scowls at me, his hand moving to the hilt of the sword at his waist—*my* sword, I realize.

"What are you doing?" they both ask.

"I am not leaving without Rowan," I say, slicing into the thick vines wrapped around Rowan's arms and torso.

"Haléndal, no!" Rowan says. "I will stay. It is my penance. I will pay for what I have done. I only wish for the safety of you and your sister."

Lifií moves toward me, and I move quickly to Rowan's other side, slicing through another vine.

"You must listen to me, Lifií," I say. "My people are searching for your home as we speak. If they find you, they will bring more warriors and attack. We outnumber the elves by nearly two to one. You would not stand a chance." I slice through the third vine as I continue, "However, if we three are all returned by an elf who wishes to help, our village head may relent and call back the men and women doing reconnaissance in the area. As I promised before, our village leaders will punish Rowan—*severely*. You can be certain of that. He has caused tension between our races, and they will not appreciate that." I slice through the last vine around Rowan's torso and move to the vine binding his wrists together.

Thus far, Lifií seems to be listening to me. He has yet to attempt to stop me. He shakes his head and looks away, frustrated. "My father will…" He does not finish his sentence.

I stop what I am doing and look at him. "What will your father do to you, exactly? You say he will beat you, but how? With what?"

Gwen gasps again, and Lifií's jaw tightens.

"I do not wish to reveal my people's methods of punishment to humans," he says.

I raise an eyebrow at him. "You already have! You told me that he would beat you."

Lifií looks at me for a long time, holding my gaze in indecision before sighing and admitting, "He will use a whip. Perhaps other things. Whatever he feels is necessary. Everyone will watch. I must be made an example of what happens when someone frees my father's prisoners."

I hesitate, unable to comprehend the cruelty. Some humans have been beaten with whips, but only in extreme situations, and no one has been forced to watch.

As if he can read my thoughts, Lifií says, "My people are different from yours. We are larger and stronger. We can endure a strict beating."

When I still do not respond, Lifií says, "I knew this would happen when I agreed to help. I decided that letting your sister go free is worth the retribution. She has done nothing amiss. But my people will want to punish Rowan themselves."

"You are the one whom Rowan has wronged," I point out. "If you are willing to let him go and be punished by his village leaders, does that mean nothing to your father and people?"

Lifií stands still, holding my gaze again. Finally, he pushes his brown hair from his forehead and turns away. "Bring him," he says, his voice soft. "I will do this for you, Haléndal."

I am surprised that he remembers my name. He has only heard it mentioned a couple of times. I watch him in silence as he moves to the gate, peering out into the stone-walled corridor to be certain we are still alone. I do not understand why hearing him say my name rattles me as much as it does. It makes me feel warm inside. I shake myself and finish cutting through the vine around Rowan's wrists.

Rowan groans with relief and rises to his feet. He and Gwen both wrap their arms around me gratefully. I put my left arm around my sister, but I do not return Rowan's hug. I am angry with him for his actions toward Lifií and for bringing this enmity between our people and the elves. Rowan and Gwen step away, and Rowan begins rubbing his arms and hands.

Lifíí motions us to come to him. Silent as mice, Rowan, Gwen, and I move across the prison floor to the gate and peer into the passageway.

Lifíí looks at us. "I have Haléndal's sword, but I cannot return Rowan's or…yours." He points to my sister. He probably does not recall Gwen's name. "I do not know where my people took them, and I could not ask anyone, as doing so might have looked suspicious. I apologize."

He steps out into the passage and points to the torch on the wall, which is barely burning. "As we come to torches, you will have to stand in the darkness as I—what is your word?—*extinguish* them. We have better vision in the dark than humans, but the less light we have, the easier it will be for us."

I was unaware that elves could see in the darkness, but I do not question Lifíí. Neither do Rowan and Gwen.

"I will hold Haléndal's hand. She will hold her sister's hand. Her sister will hold Rowan's." Lifíí curls his lip in a disgusted manner when he mentions Rowan's name. "No talking. No sounds. Silent as the forest animals. Understand?"

We all nod, and Lifíí holds his hand up, telling us to stay where we are. Carefully watching the exit to the corridor, Lifíí uses a small tin cup that was also hanging from his belt to extinguish the torch. The passage is plunged into blackness.

I reach for Gwen's hand, and I presume she reaches for Rowan's. A moment later, I feel Lifií's fingers slide easily between mine. He did not even need to grope in the darkness for my hand. Elves must truly be able to see, no matter how little light there is. I wonder what that must be like.

I shiver at Lifií's touch. I have never held hands with a young man, much less a large, well-muscled elf. I remember the times when he gently reached out to touch my blonde curls, and I must force the memories from my mind. *Focus, Haléndal!* I tell myself. *We must escape!*

Lifií leads us down the corridor and into the enormous main cavern. He releases my hand and extinguishes two torches that are still burning slightly. He comes back to me in the darkness, and we continue in this manner, slipping silently through the passages of the cave. The only sound is the occasional scrape of a boot and the soft thud of Lifií's staff hitting the ground as he uses it to help him walk. We rarely bump into a wall, as Lifií can see well enough to keep us from doing such things.

We approach the main entrance, and moonlight streams into the cave through the false trees and shrubbery covering the door. I feel ecstatic and apprehensive, unable to believe we have made it this far without being discovered.

Lifií pulls his hand from mine and edges stealthily to the opening in the stone wall. He flattens his back against the wall and peers around it.

I can only just see the arm of the elf guarding the opening from the outside.

Lifií holds up his hand, reminding us to stay where we are, and then he steps quickly through the opening, leaving his walking stick behind him against the wall. There is a startled exclamation, but Lifií covers the guard's mouth with his hand and attempts to choke him.

However, the elf is strong and fights harder than Lifií anticipated. Thankfully, the elf does not call out for help, as he is focused on grappling with Lifií. In a moment, the strange elf has Lifií trapped beneath him on the ground.

I see a movement to my right and glance up to see someone pass me. It is Rowan! What is he doing? I reach for him but miss as he steps through the cave opening.

The elf on top of Lifií pauses as he recognizes his opponent in the moonlight. "Lifií!" he says in surprise.

At that moment, Rowan strikes. He hits the guard's jaw with an upward strike. The elf's head jerks backward, and his body immediately sags to the ground, unconscious. He must not have seen Rowan approaching.

I stare at Rowan, shocked. I have never seen Rowan fight with his fists, though I know he has a history of drunken tavern fights. He knocked the elf into unconsciousness with only one strike!

Lifií stares at Rowan as well and then turns his wide eyes to the body on top of his legs. "What are you doing?" he hisses, his voice angry. "I told you to stay back! I did not need you!"

He slides out from under the elf guard but sucks in a pained breath as he does so. Pulling his broken leg to him, he clenches his teeth, breathing through the pain from fighting the elf. The fight clearly aggravated his injury further.

Rowan gives a soft snort. "You needed me. You were fighting with a broken leg! I was only attempting to help!"

Lifií gives Rowan a poisonous glare. "You have no idea what you have done! I am already going to be punished. You are only adding to the grievances that my people have against you. If you are unwilling to comply when I tell you to stand back, I should not be taking you with us! You will only cause more problems!"

Rowan does not know what to say to that. He looks down at the unconscious elf on the ground. "I apologize. I did not intend to..." He seems unsure how to finish his sentence.

Gwen and I step through the opening. Lifií holds his hand out to me. I grasp his hand and grip the nearest tree to brace myself. It seems to be a real tree trunk, but Lifií told me these trees are fake. I do not understand. I pull Lifií up.

Lifií stands on his one good leg and points to the cave entrance. "I need my staff," he whispers.

I step back into the cave to retrieve it, but as I reach out to take it, another hand also reaches for it. My heart stops, and I raise my head to see another elf standing on the other side of the stick, only slightly illuminated by the moonlight. It is the elven elder!

CHAPTER 8

I squeal in surprise and fear, and I lunge for the opening again. I am followed by the elder who is holding Lifií's walking stick.

Lifií's expression turns to dread.

I move quickly to his side and grasp his hand. I do not know why I do this, but Lifií does not pull away.

He squeezes my hand instead. "I tried," he whispers. "I truly tried to release all of you."

I believe him, and my heart aches with the knowledge that he will soon suffer much more pain than I have ever experienced. And what will happen to Rowan, Gwen, and me? Will we be forced to serve the elven elder?

The elder steps out into the moonlight. "Lifií," he says with a stern glare.

"*Evantiidgh*," Lifií answers, his head lowered in respect.

The elder's eyes roam over us humans and settle on his son once more as elven men and women appear in the opening of the cave. There are only about ten elves, but they are armed with swords and spears, and Lifií is the only one of us who has a sword. We are outnumbered.

The elder looks down at the unconscious body of the elven guard and spits on him angrily. He is likely angry that a human could beat an elf so quickly. The elder says something to Lifií in his language.

Lifií winces. "He says he was suspicious of me and my story from the beginning," he whispers. "Especially since I did not want to have a battle in Kaahl or to bring your sister here."

The elder speaks again, motioning to the people behind him, doubtlessly stressing the fact that we are outnumbered. Attempting to run would be a point-less and perhaps fatal mistake. As the elder continues to speak, his son becomes more and more agitated by my side.

The elf guard that Rowan knocked out groans and stirs. When Lifií moves to help the elf, the elder barks out a curt order. Lifií steps back, and another elf comes from behind the elder to pull the guard through the crowd and into the cave.

Finally, Lifií speaks, unable to hold his frustra-tion any longer. His words come in an angry rush, and I notice his head is no longer lowered. He looks his father in the eye as he speaks to him in a manner that I would never dare speak to my father or mother, much less to one of our leaders.

The elder scowls and the angry conversation continues. Eventually, Lifií is forced to lean back against the trunk of the tree behind us, as the elder is still holding the staff.

I glance at Rowan and Gwen. Rowan's arm is draped protectively around my sister's shoulders, and Gwen clings to Rowan in fear. While in the prison, Gwen told Rowan and me that she was confused. She still loves Rowan very much, but she is also both surprised and angry about the wrongs that he has done. She is uncertain whether she can marry Rowan, knowing the great evil he has brought upon our people. He is to blame for the deaths of humans and elves in the battle in Kaahl's square. At this moment, however, she seems to be relying on his strength.

I eventually shake Lifii's hand, hard enough to get his attention. He looks down at me.

"What is going on?" I ask. "What is he saying?"

Lifii glances briefly at his father and then looks back at me. "He is telling me all the terrible things he will do to all of us." He rolls his eyes up at the leaves and branches above our heads in an annoyed manner. "I am telling him what you said—that your sister was in a marriage ceremony and is not a village leader, how your leaders will punish Rowan, and that returning you all to Kaahl will avoid more animosity between our people and yours."

"Does he believe you?" I ask.

Lifii shrugs as the elder folds his arms across his massive chest and barks something in his language again. Lifii's eyebrows rise, and he asks a question.

His father makes a dismissive motion with his hands, saying something else.

Lifíí's shoulders sag slightly, but he nods and pulls his hand from mine. "Go!" he says. "My father has agreed to release you all. If I am willing to release Rowan, even though I am the one he injured, my father says that he will stay out of my decision."

Rowan and Gwen slowly step backward, farther from the cave entrance. I stand in uncertainty, but Lifíí gives me a small smile and motions for me to leave.

"It will be all right," he assures me. "Go to Kaahl." He then adds, "And many thanks for helping me with my leg."

"I…you're welcome," I respond.

I turn to follow my sister and Rowan, who have disappeared through the veil of false trees. As I do, I feel nauseated. Something does not seem right.

I step around the first tree and look back. Lifíí is looking at his father, head held high and shoulders back. It is false bravery. The elder motions for Lifíí to come to him even though Lifíí still does not have his walking stick. As Lifíí painfully hobbles toward his father, I remember what he said about the probability of a serious beating.

I recall the feeling I had in the forest when I saw Lifíí underneath the fallen tree trunk—the feeling that kept me from simply leaving him to his fate. The same feeling courses through me now. I cannot leave him to his imminent beating, but I do not know how to stop it.

I glance toward the cave entrance and see that no one is watching me. The elves are too intent on what is happening between their elder and his son.

The elder gives some curt commands, and two elven men step forward. One uses another strong vine to bind Lifíí's hands to a strong iron rod that is protruding from the stone wall near the cave entrance. The second elf stands by, his hand on the hilt of a sword hanging from his belt, as though he expects Lifíí to fight against his punishment.

Lifíí does not fight. He allows what is happening in silence, his head lowered.

Someone grabs my arm, startling me. It is Gwen. She gestures with her head for me to follow her.

I hesitate, taking another look at Lifíí. His father says some more words, then he enters the cave, walking away from his son. The other elves follow him, except for one elven woman, who takes the first guard's place on the opposite side of the cave opening from where Lifíí stands.

When everyone else is gone, Lifíí painfully moves until he can sit on the grass, though the rod to which his hands are tied is now above his head.

Gwen shakes my arm more vigorously, and I know that I should leave. It appears the elves are waiting until morning to follow through on Lifíí's penalty for setting the captives free. Lifíí must spend the remainder of the night in this uncomfortable place, awaiting judgment.

I turn with great reluctance and follow Gwen through the trees. The guard makes an exclamation when she sees us, but upon realizing that we are only the people set free and that we are leaving, she settles back into her watch without incident.

Gwen and I meet Rowan, and we move through the trees. However, we are not entirely certain which direction we came from, and the tree branches above us block our view of the stars. We walk straight and eventually find our way to a forest trail. After a short argument between Rowan and Gwen about which direction to go, they agree to turn to the right.

I do not follow them. Instead, I hesitate, looking back in the direction from which we came. My heart seems to be torn in two.

I cannot leave him. I cannot leave him. I cannot leave him!

CHAPTER 9

"You two go on to Kaahl," I say. "I am going back to the cave."

Gwen looks at me as though I am growing dragon wings. "What? Haléndal, you cannot go back! Why would you do such a thing?"

I look behind me again. I cannot leave him. "I…I must help. I must find out if there is something I can do. I…"

I do not know how to explain the urge to return to the elven cave and attempt another rescue. It is possible that Lifií will not even want me to rescue him. He knew that he would be beaten when he agreed to help me. If I can free him, what will happen then? Will he be able to return to his people? Will the elves ever accept him back if he leaves before accepting his whipping?

"Haléndal," Rowan says, his voice urgent, "please reconsider. You have no sword. Neither Gwen nor I have a sword to loan to you. There is a new guard at the cave. There is nothing you can do for Lifií."

I step back into the trees. "You go on to Kaahl," I say again. "I'm going back."

"Haléndal!" My sister is nearly beside herself. "Please, don't! What are *we* supposed to do?"

"Getting Rowan back to the leaders of Kaahl is important," I tell her. "That was the promise we made to Lifíí. Go. I will be all right."

Without awaiting another response, I turn and hurry back the way I came, through the trees. I hear another protest as I leave, but I pay no heed.

Within a few minutes, I slow down to a walk, choosing with great care where I place my feet so as not to step on a twig and make a loud noise.

I am soon near the cave. I stand a distance away, not wanting to alert the guard. My heart breaks as I watch Lifíí try to get some sleep on the ground with his arms stretched above his head. He looks very uncomfortable. I also have not forgotten that his leg is broken. After all the time he has spent helping me, my sister, and, begrudgingly, Rowan, I can imagine that his leg is in immense pain. He has not given the bone any time to heal. He has been moving far too much today.

My eyes move to the female elven guard. Her sharp eyes carefully watch the trees for any sign of trouble. She seems to have seen me a few times, but as I prepare to turn and flee, her eyes continue their scan.

As I watch Lifíí and his guard, I realize that if I am to free Lifíí, he will need another walking stick. I slip quietly farther into the trees and prepare another staff for him to lean on. I return to my post. I am nearer to the guard than to Lifií, though I am unsure if this is a wise position. I will have to pass the guard to approach Lifií or circle the area in a wide arc to avoid being seen.

As I keep a quiet watch on the scene, studying every angle to find a way to rescue the handsome young elf who has done so much to help me, it begins to rain. Within moments, I am soaked and miserable. I try to ignore the discomfort.

After standing in the rain for nearly an hour, I suddenly realize that I may have the chance that I have been waiting for. The elven woman keeping watch yawns and sinks to the ground, leaning against the cliff wall. I watch, both apprehensive and excited, as she slowly nods off to sleep.

I make my move. I circle the area, taking painfully slow, deliberate steps, and approach Lifií from his right side. He, too, is nodding off despite the misery he must be in. I squat beside him and touch his arm.

Lifií's head snaps up, and he lets out a startled sound.

I cringe and look at the guard. She is still asleep. I have never been so grateful for the soothing sound of the rain!

"Haléndal!" Lifií whispers, bewildered. "What are you doing here?"

I keep an eye on the guard as I respond, my voice also low. "I want to help. You are in this predicament because of me, because I insisted on releasing

Gwen. You still have my sword. Allow me to cut you free. You can leave with me."

Lifií's gaze turns to something I do not know how to describe. Perhaps tenderness? He gives me a sad smile. "Haléndal, you should not have come here. I shall be all right. These punishments happen more often than you may realize. We endure them, and then we are taken directly to our healer. We are—how do you say it?—*ourselves* within a few days, though I shall have many more days of healing before my leg is well."

"Have *you* ever been beaten in this manner?" I ask.

Lifií hesitates. "Not as serious as this will be, but I shall be all right. Haléndal, you must go. If my father catches you here…" He turns his head to look at the cave entrance, which is still empty.

I look at the sleeping guard. She stirs a bit and mumbles something. She is still sleeping.

"I cannot make myself leave," I say. A tear slides down my cheek, revealing the feelings of my heart being rent in two. "Lifií, I…"

Another tear slides down, and Lifií moves enough to catch the tear with his elbow. I know the tender look in his eyes. He would catch the tears with his fingers if he could…or perhaps he would touch my rain-soaked curls instead.

"No weeping," he says softly. "I shall be fine. If I leave with you, I shall never be allowed to return to my home and my people. I do not wish to leave them forever. I shall accept this as retribution for what I have done. It is all right."

I was afraid of that possibility. More tears blur my vision, and I squeeze my eyes shut, forcing the tears down my face so I can see clearly.

"You are a brave elf," I say.

"You are a brave human," he responds. "Now, leave before you are seen."

I start to stand, but I stop myself. "Will I ever see you again?"

"I…we can meet," he says. "After I am healed."

"Perhaps in a fortnight?" I suggest. "At the place of the fallen oak trees—chinífia trees, as your people call them."

"What is 'fortnight'?" Lifií asks in confusion.

"Two weeks."

When Lifií still appears confused, I try again to clarify. "Fourteen days?"

He nods. "I shall see you then when the morning sun is just coming over the mountain."

I give him as much of a smile as I can. "I shall see you then."

I glance at the guard, stand, and prepare to leave. However, I first stoop and unfasten my sword belt from Lifií's waist. It feels good to have my familiar sword and scabbard back. Lifií does not try to stop me. Before standing, I press my lips to Lifií's forehead. It is not a kiss, but it is the closest that I can give.

Lifií looks surprised, but his face then breaks into a smile. "Goodbye, Haléndal."

"Goodbye, Lifíí."

I turn and slip away through the trees to the quiet sound of the rain on the leaves and grass. I realize that the second staff I made was never used. I leave it behind me and set my course toward the forest path and the village of Kaahl.

CHAPTER 10

Two weeks later, I hurry down the same forested mountain path I traveled when I first met Lifií. I carry in my satchel two blueberry pastries that I made for breakfast this morning. I made an extra pastry to bring to Lifií. I did not tell my mother or family I was meeting Lifií, as they might disapprove. I did ask for permission to take a morning walk and eat my breakfast in the beauty of the forest. Mother agreed, saying that I must return within two hours to begin my chores.

As I approach the oak grove beside the trail, I feel my heart sinking. I do not see Lifií anywhere nearby. I shall wait for him. I sit on the log that was once on top of Lifií's leg and wait. After quite some time, I begin to wonder if he has forgotten to come.

Then I feel a gentle hand on my shoulder. I am unable to keep the smile from my face. I turn and raise my eyes, finding a pair of captivating green eyes above me.

"Hello, Haléndal," Lifií says, his voice soft in the quiet of the forest. He leans the walking stick that I gave him against a stump.

"Hello." I stand quickly, taking his hand in mine and looking him over as if checking for signs of the beating that he took. "You look well."

"You look lovely as well," Lifií says. He blushes when the words leave his mouth, and so do I. "I meant to say you look well," he tries to clarify.

I smile and squeeze his hand. "How are you doing?"

"I am well. I no longer have to wear bandages around my…" He hesitates, motioning toward his torso with his free hand, unable to think of the correct word in my language. "Also, my leg seems to be healing nicely."

I reach out to touch his side with my hand. "May I see?" I blush again, realizing what that question sounds like. "I just want to…ease my mind, I suppose."

Lifií nods. He slips his hand from mine and turns his back to me. He raises his odd, leafy tunic.

I gape at his bare back, feeling my heart twist. Lifií has many long stripes across his back. Some are scabbed over; others have completely healed, leaving only scars. I reach out to touch a scar, following its jagged line with my finger.

"I'm so sorry you had to go through that," I say, my voice catching in my throat.

Lifií pulls his tunic back down, smoothing it over his hips as he turns to face me. He smiles. "I am well, Haléndal," he assures me. "Do not worry. It was painful, but I accepted it and took it better than I expected."

When I do not respond, Lifií changes the subject of our conversation. "How are your sister and… Rowan?"

"Gwen is all right. As you can imagine, she has been rather emotional these last few days. The man she agreed to marry made some terrible mistakes."

I fidget as I remember the nights I have heard her quiet sobs drifting across the room.

"Rowan is…as good as expected, I suppose. He was given three nights in the stocks and two more in our prison, and now he has hard work to accomplish in our village. He works from dawn until dusk every day, under strict supervision, and spends each night in prison. This will go on for months to come."

Lifií processes the man's punishment in silence, as if trying to decide whether Rowan will truly learn his lesson. "What are 'stocks'?"

I describe the stocks to Lifií. Our stocks are in the prison yard, but many people walk by there every day. Rowan has been sufficiently humiliated; that much is certain. He had to stand with his neck and wrists locked in the stocks for three days and nights straight. I cannot imagine how uncomfortable he must have been.

Lifií nods when I finish my explanation. "I see. And what of Gwen? The marriage, I mean. Will she still marry him?"

I do not know how to answer him. "I don't know," I admit. "They are still in love, but Gwen must decide if she is willing to overlook Rowan's wrongdoings. I can say that Rowan truly seems to have repented. He admitted to everything he did and accepted his punishment without the slightest complaint. Time will show us what Gwen decides. Right now, people are very angry with Rowan. They openly scorn him and even spit on him as he works. They are grieving and angry about the deaths that occurred when the elves attacked Kaahl. Rowan takes it all without complaint, but Gwen has to decide if she will accept the scorn that may transfer to her if she marries him." I shrug.

Lifií reaches for my hand and slides his fingers through mine. "It will be all right. Everything will work out as it should." He pauses before adding, "I have decided to try to—what is your word?—*forgive* Rowan for what he did. I am reminded of him when pain shoots through my leg, but I try to shove the thoughts away and move on. I believe we can all move on if he stays away from my people to avoid the temptation to do something like this again. I will tell my father about Rowan's penalties to set his mind at ease. He is unsure if Rowan will continue to be a problem in the future."

I nod, understanding. We are quiet for a moment, and I must admit that I am thoroughly enjoying the feeling of Lifií's hand holding mine.

Lifií pulls my hand up and looks at it as if hearing my thoughts. His hand is so much larger than mine that the size difference can be likened to a lizard's foot next to that of a dragon. He rubs his fingers across the palm of my hand, making me shiver.

I need a distraction.

"I brought something for you," I say, holding up my satchel shyly.

Lifií's eyebrows rise. "What is it?"

I open the satchel and remove the pastries wrapped in paper. The smell of blueberries joins the scents of the forest. "I brought my breakfast to eat in the forest and extra for you if you want it."

Lifií's face breaks into a smile. "It smells delicious. What is it?"

I give a detailed description of the pastry's ingredients as I help Lifií sit on the fallen oak log. I say a blessing over the food and watch as Lifií takes his first bite.

His eyes widen with delight, and he eats the remainder so quickly that I only have time to take a few bites. I laugh as he wipes crumbs from his face with the hem of his tunic.

"That was as delicious as it smelled!" he exclaims, making me blush.

As I take another bite, Lifií reaches over and pinches a small piece off the other end of my pastry. He shoves it into his mouth before I can stop him.

"Hey!" I laugh.

Lifií smiles and moves his hand up to gently squeeze my upper arm. "How is the sword wound?"

"Fine," I say. "Only a scar now. I would show it to you, but these laces on my sleeves make pulling the sleeve up difficult."

Lifií smiles. His eyes roam over my face, and he raises his hand to touch a blonde curl.

I remember that the first time he did this I had to resist the temptation to touch the tip of his pointed ears. I hesitate now but give in and reach up to feel his ear.

Lifií chuckles, the sound warm in the cool morning air. He moves his other hand to touch my own ear. His hands are now cupping each side of my face.

I find myself hoping for a kiss, though I have never been the type to desire such things.

Lifií does not kiss me, but he bends down and presses his lips to my forehead, as I did to him when he was tied to the rod outside his home.

I realize that I am closing my eyes, soaking in the delightful feeling of his lips against my skin. I also realize that I forgot to eat the rest of my pastry. I leave it on my lap, greatly enjoying my time with Lifií.

"I must go," he whispers.

I am disappointed, but before we part ways, we set another time to meet. He smiles and waves as he reenters the forest trees, and I return to the path that leads home. Lifií must return to his people and I to mine.

The days ahead may be full of uncertainties, but I will always be glad that I stopped to help the tall, muscular forest elf trapped beneath a fallen tree by the mountain trail.

End

ABOUT THE AUTHOR

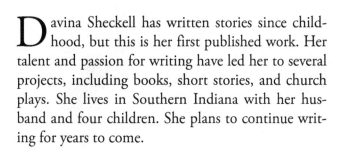

Davina Sheckell has written stories since childhood, but this is her first published work. Her talent and passion for writing have led her to several projects, including books, short stories, and church plays. She lives in Southern Indiana with her husband and four children. She plans to continue writing for years to come.